For SNate, who's got all the right moves

A Random House Australia book
Published by Random House Australia Pty Ltd
Level 3, 100 Pacific Highway, North Sydney NSW 2060
www.randomhouse.com.au

First published by Random House Australia in 2015

Addresses for companies within the Random House Group can be found at
www.randomhouse.com.au/offices

National Library of Australia
Cataloguing-in-Publication Entry

Author: Bound, Samantha-Ellen
Title: Hit the streets
ISBN: 978 0 857982 841 (pbk)
Series: Silver shoes; 2
Target Audience: For primary-school age
Subjects: Girls – Juvenile fiction
                 Dance – Juvenile fiction
                 Dance schools – Juvenile fiction
                 Family crises – Juvenile fiction
Dewey Number: A823.4

Cover and internal illustrations by J.Yi
Cover design by Kirby Armstrong
Internal design by Midland Typesetters, Australia
Printed in Australia by Griffin Press, an accredited ISO AS/NZS 14001:2004
Environmental Management System printer

Random House Australia uses papers that are natural, renewable and recyclable
products and made from wood grown in sustainable forests. The logging and
manufacturing processes are expected to conform to the environmental regulations
of the country of origin.

Hit the Streets

SAMANTHA-ELLEN BOUND

RANDOM HOUSE AUSTRALIA

Chapter One

Four o'clock.

There was nothing else for it. I couldn't put it off any longer.

I'd dawdled all the way to Silver Shoes, but now I was here, ready to try my first hip hop class.

My stomach felt funny, sort of inside out. I'd been excited all week but suddenly my shoes weren't new enough, my hair wasn't cool enough, and I was sure my hip hop moves would totally blow.

My name's Ashley Jenkyns, by the way. I've only been going to Silver Shoes for a couple of months. Before that I went to Dance Art Academy. I don't really miss it, though – especially some of the girls there!

I love Silver Shoes. The teachers are fun and friendly, and the dark halls and cramped corners feel cosy and welcoming. There's always something happening here.

Like when I stood in front of those big double doors leading into Silver Shoes. Half of my body was tingling with excitement and the other half was so nervous and whispering things at me like, 'Go home, Ashley, you're gonna be no good.'

But I wouldn't know if I didn't try.

I crept to the change room to get into my dance gear. Yuck. My Chucks were looking a bit tatty. I hope no one noticed.

I've wanted to try hip hop for sooooo long! Dance Art never ran hip hop classes. I guess it was too 'improper' for them. They have their noses stuck up in the clouds over there.

It's pretty scary when you try a new style or class for the first time. I don't mind making a clown of myself, as long as it's on purpose. So I didn't want to turn up and look silly or not fit in. Or worse, have all the attention on me. That's what happened when I first came to Silver Shoes. There was this jazz audition and one of the dancers, my friend Ellie, fell over and glared at me like it was my fault.

But we're okay, now. Most of the time. She's one of my best friends at Silver Shoes, along with Riley and Paige.

I wished they were here with me now, eating lolly snakes and making jokes. But we all have our favourite styles: Ellie loves jazz, ballet is Riley's thing, and lately Paige has been getting into ballroom. Hip hop is my style – at least, I hoped it would be.

I'll tell you why I love it.

My sister, Bridget, has this boyfriend and he calls himself Brimax. They're both eighteen. When I was little (well, it was about two years ago, so little-ish) I asked him why he had such a stupid name. After Bridget yelled at me for being rude (I don't know why, Brimax found it funny), he told me it was his stage name.

'Stage name? Why do you have a stage name?' I asked.

'Because I'm a dancer,' he said.

'I'm a dancer and I don't have a stage name,' I said.

'It's my breakdancing name,' he told me. 'My real name's Brian. But after a while, when they get to know your style, your crew will always pick out a name for you.'

'What would my stage name be?' I asked.

'Annoyanator,' said Bridget.

'AshFunK,' he said.

'Cool. What are some of your moves?' I asked him.

He showed me, right there beside the kitchen table. Wow. At Dance Art we'd been in the middle of lots of boring training for our classical exams, which kind of sucked, so when he showed me all these acrobatic, hard-hitting moves, I thought it was amazing.

'That was *so* cool,' I said.

'You want to come watch a battle?' he asked me.

'No, she doesn't,' said Bridget, straightaway.

'Yes,' I said, just to annoy Bridget.

So that weekend we went to this gig where Brimax and his crew were performing. Really I think Bridget liked having me there, because she kept holding my hand and telling me not to leave her alone.

I wasn't going anywhere! The dancing was the best thing I'd seen in ages. It was like what you'd see on hip hop and pop video clips and everyone looked like they were having a blast. Pointed feet and straight backs seemed to be the last thing on anyone's mind.

The music was loud, people were doing amazing tricks and busting out funky moves. There was massive energy everywhere.

I knew I'd found my style.

But I didn't have a chance to try the classes until I came to Silver Shoes. They do trial classes for free where you can see if you like the style enough to sign up for the term.

So finally, *finally*, here I was! Dressed and ready for the class. No more putting it off.

I took a big breath and walked out of the change room and towards studio two. Then I pushed open the door and went in.

Chapter Two

Hip hop music thumped towards me and there was a group over in the corner trying to spin on their heads.

I slouched in the doorway, trying to stand like how I imagined a hip hop dancer would stand. Clearly I got it all wrong, because no one even looked at me.

Way to go, AshFunK.

I swaggered (but really stumbled) over

to the side of the room where everyone was waiting around to start.

Jay, the hip hop teacher, looked up from where he was flicking through his iPod. He gave me a big grin. My friend Paige would have died right then. She has the biggest crush on him. He's super tall and has the friendliest smile and the biggest brown eyes. If Paige sees him in the halls walking by and flicking his long hair off his face, she squeaks and suddenly finds the floor very interesting.

'Hey Ash,' he said, coming over.

'Hey,' I said, and tried to think of something cool to say. My brain hummed like our fridge when you open it late at night.

'Awesome to see you in class,' he said.

'Thought I'd show you how it's done,' I joked.

'Well, you've brought the right attitude.' Jay laughed.

'Now I just have to try not to fall on my face,' I said.

'Hey,' said Jay, 'even if you do, own it. Nobody ever knows any different. That's what hip hop's all about – putting your own personal style on it.'

'Look at me,' I said. 'Do I look like I have much style?'

My t-shirt was this holey hand-me-down from Bridget. It was still too big and said 'Sun Surf Sand' on the front.

'Totally stylin'.' Jay grinned.

I laughed.

'Come on,' he said, herding me over to the dance floor. 'Don't be shy. Stay at the back to start with if you want, to get a feel for it.'

I headed to the back. There were more boys in hip hop than there were in jazz class. I felt a bit more at home here than I did when surrounded by prim and proper girls in pink leotards. I'm kind of a tomboy outside dance class. I like surfing, scuba and going out on my uncle's boat. If I'm not dancing, I'm in the water. I even have a plush turtle as my dancing good luck charm!

There were a few people I hadn't seen around Silver Shoes before. I spotted Serah, though, who was in my jazz class.

I also saw Tove.

Tove is the closest friend of Jasmine de Lacy, who's probably one of the best dancers at Silver Shoes. You know how I was talking about Ellie? Well, Jasmine is Ellie's number one dance enemy, which means she is also the enemy of Ellie's friends.

Tove was trying very hard not to look my way. Jasmine always made a point of saying hip hop was not a true dance style. I wondered what she'd say if she knew Tove was here doing hip hop.

We started to warm up and stretch. I began to relax. A lot of people find warm-up boring, but I like it. There's no competition or pressure to learn anything, you can just loosen up to awesome music and get in the zone.

I love hip hop tunes. I even love them when Brimax comes over to see Bridget and cranks them up loud enough to hear from five houses down the street.

Jay got us working our hips and stomach. First our hips were going left to right, then front to back, then circling, then swaying. Next Jay made us shake our bums in all these different ways! Everyone started laughing. I was really enjoying myself, especially when I saw how much Tove seemed to like shaking her bottom around. We did lots of chest and back isolations, and then we went through stretches that made our shoulders and neck loose.

'Get loose, get loose,' Jay said, making a sign with his hand. Then he turned his hand upside down. 'But not too loose!'

Everyone laughed. I guess it was a personal joke in class.

Before we learnt the weekly choreography, Jay got us doing all these moves that he said were 'essential if you're gonna be a stylin' hip hopper'. He set his iPod to a hip hop megamix and then we hit the floor. Jay called them out as he took us through them: 'jerk', 'lock', 'walk-it-out', 'reebok', 'wopping', 'cranking', 'kick step' and then some silly, fun ones like the 'running man' and 'the wave'. Everybody took to the moves like they'd done them a hundred times, while I was falling over my own feet and my body made these weird angles that weren't "stylin'" at all.

I won't lie – I was totally awkward when I first started. I kept catching myself out, sitting

too high in the steps and being too formal like I was still in jazz-ballet. But then I got to know the flow and rhythm of the moves, and I listened to the music and began to find my groove.

And then the best part – we learnt the dance!

Chapter Three

That was when the magic really happened.

Jay picked a Chris Brown song called 'I Can Transform Ya'. It had all these robotic tones and a pounding electro beat. Jay called it 'robo-crunk'.

We weren't doing robot moves or anything like that, though. Jay's choreography was based around the idea of being a ninja, and he teamed it with lots of isolations and footwork right into the ground.

As we learnt the choreography, I forgot that I was the 'new girl' at Silver Shoes, or that I'd never done hip hop before. I forgot that there was a hole in my tights and that my technique in other classes always held me back from getting put in the front row.

Technique may have been important, but Jay had this thing about 'hitting it'.

'When you slide and pop into this position, *hit it*,' he'd say. Or, 'When you drop to the floor, I want you to *hit it*.'

Or when we had to pause and then look to the front, he'd go, 'This move is all about being on top of the beat, letting the music pull your head forward and then bam, you *hit it* – you land that beat and throw it away to the audience.'

When he watched us perform the choreography he'd just taught us, he would point at someone who did really well and yell out, 'Yeah! You *hit that*!'

But it didn't make the rest of us feel bad, or like we hadn't done well. Sometimes that happens in jazz class when Miss Caroline praises Jasmine. That always makes Ellie huff and puff like a dragon.

What I liked best, though, was that Jay didn't choreograph to counts. Everything wasn't 1, 2, 3, 4, with a move to go with it. Jay's style followed the rhythm and mood of the song, where a sound effect or word would be used to showcase a move, even if it didn't fit within the regular beats of the music. And we were allowed to add our own 'flava' to it.

'What you wanna do is highlight the moment the beat creates,' Jay said. 'That way, it's more about expressing yourself rather than just getting all the steps.'

Jay was a cool teacher. I love Miss Caroline, of course. Miss Caroline owns Silver Shoes, and she teaches a lot of the classes. But Jay was like a fun big brother, which I liked, because I only have Bridget. He reminded me a bit of Brimax. I'm pretty sure they've danced in the same crew before.

'Nice one,' Jay said to me after the class, when everyone was cooling down or getting a drink. 'I saw you hitting it. Who would have thought little Ash could bring it like that, hey? Miss Caroline would have a heart attack!'

'I *loved* your class,' I said, standing up.

'Put it there,' said Jay, holding out a hand for me to high five. 'So how'd you go? A lot of people think hip hop isn't technical, yeah, because you can use so much freestyle. But it's hard work, am I right?'

'Heaps,' I said. 'Just as hard as doing an amazing jeté while keeping perfect pointe!'

'We've got our own technique,' Jay said. 'You gotta have that stance, that flow, that flavour. And then you've got transitions, flexibility, tricks, isolations, footwork.'

'Yeah,' I said. 'Might need to work on a few of those.'

'I hope so,' Jay said. 'You're coming back, right?'

I decided at that moment to be hopeful. 'Sure,' I said.

Ugh. I imagined the conversation over dinner tonight. I already knew it wouldn't be as simple as that.

'Excellent,' said Jay. 'Ash in the house!'

'Ash Attack!' I said.

'Smashley,' Jay said.

'AshFunk.'

'Smashin' Ash!'

'An Ashley a Day Keeps the Doctor Away,' I said.

'Hmm,' teased Jay. 'Too long. Not your best.'

'I'll work on it,' I said.

I ran into Tove as I was leaving Silver Shoes. 'Oh, hi,' I said. 'Sorry.'

'That's okay,' she said, and pointed at the wall. 'Did you see that? Danceworks are running a competition to be the face of their new hip hop dancewear range. They want real dancers!'

'Do you have attitude? All the right moves?' I read off the poster. 'Be the face of our new "Freestyle" dance range and win a whole new Danceworks wardrobe.'

'How amazing would that be,' Tove said.

Gosh. If anyone needed a new dance wardrobe, it was me.

'Yeah,' I said, walking with her. 'Hey, it was cool to see you in hip hop class today. You were really good. You should totally enter the competition.'

'Thanks,' said Tove. She switched her bag to the other shoulder and smiled at me. 'You should too.'

'Ha,' I laughed. 'I'll break the camera.'

When we rounded the corner, Jasmine's mum was sitting behind the reception desk. Tove's face glazed over and she went back to her 'Jasmine's number one sidekick' face.

'See you in class,' she sniffed, before running over to Mrs de Lacy, who gave her a huge perfumed hug and cried, 'Tovey! How was your solo lesson? I hope you're hungry. Jazzy wants to go to Groove Train for dinner.'

I had a feeling my dinner would be nowhere near as exciting.

Chapter Four

Hmm.

Tomatoes. Bacon. Pasta. Mum's favourite 'I'm working late, and this was cheap and easy' meal.

Wait, I think she'd shoved a bit of corn in there, too.

Welcome to dinner at the Jenkyns house.

'So, the trial class was really fun,' I said, chasing some bacon under a pile of penne.

'Oh, that's good,' said Mum. She looked really tired tonight. You could carry the shopping in the bags under her eyes.

She'd been working reception and office work at the country club and I knew she didn't really like it. But I guess she had to, now that her and Dad's landscaping business had gone bust.

'I think it's a style I could really get into,' I said.

'That's great, Ashley,' said Dad.

'Jay was saying there'd even be the chance to join crews and go in competitions and all that,' I continued. 'But they don't call them competitions, they call them battles.'

My pasta was getting cold. I felt a bit sick, anyway. There was this big gluggy lump in my throat. I call it the 'I know there's no way I'll ever get what I want' lump.

'He seems liked a nice young man,' offered Mum.

'I had the best time,' I said.

'That's great, Ash,' said Mum.

'Really great,' repeated Dad.

Everyone was silent. Bridget dropped her fork and it clanked against her bowl before falling into her cold penne.

I stared into my pasta. I took a big breath.

'I'd like to go on taking the classes,' I said.

Dad took a drink of water. Mum stared at her dinner like there was something crawling around in it. Bridget looked at me. My face got all hot.

'You know we can't afford it,' Mum said.

Another silence.

'I'm happy that you love it so much, Ash. But with you already doing two classes a week, well, it's just getting a little expensive.'

'Maybe you can drop another class,' said Bridget.

'Could you do that, Ash?' asked Dad.

'Dad!' I said. 'You know I can't! We have to take technical class if we want to be in competitions. And I can't drop jazz! My friends are there! And I'm already in the dance for the eisteddfod. And it's embarrassing!'

'Well . . .' said Dad. He took another drink of water.

'I'm sorry, Ash,' said Mum. 'It's just getting a bit pricey.'

I suppose I should tell you, but you've probably guessed. Our family doesn't have a lot of money. That's one of the reasons we moved to Bayside. And why I left Dance Art.

Mum and Dad had this gardening business – Dad built people's backyards and Mum did all the office stuff for it. But it didn't work out. We had to move house and Mum went to work at the country club. Dad is still trying to get any kind of house and garden job he can.

I guess he's not getting much because we never seem to have any money. I don't really care. Except, like now, when it means I can't dance.

Mum and Dad have always been so busy working that sometimes I don't think they notice how much I love dancing. Bridget always tells me, 'They're doing it for you, and us, Ash. You're lucky to even go to Silver Shoes, as it is!'

That's because, like I said, I was at Dance Art Academy. They are Silver Shoes' biggest competition. There's been a rivalry for ages.

A bit more about Dance Art: they're a big razzly dazzly rich school a few suburbs away. I did jazz and a few other classes there. It's expensive, though, especially around competition time, because the teachers like to go all out and have really fancy costumes.

Dance Art was cool, but I always felt like I was in the shadow of the other girls.

The girls there were a bit snooty around me because they always had the latest and greatest clothes from Danceworks or Transitions Dancewear, while I just had some five-dollar tights. Whatever. It's not like they make you dance better.

But at Silver Shoes I feel like I can do my own thing and have fun. Going to Silver Shoes has made me *love* dance, not just like it. All I need to do now is to stop being thought of as 'the new girl from the enemy dance school'.

Anyway. Now you know the back story.

'I really loved the class,' I pleaded. 'Please.'

Dad looked down at his plate. 'Sorry, Ash,' he said.

'We just can't afford it, babe,' said Mum.

I felt my throat lump get bigger and bigger. I was crushed.

Bridget sighed. 'I can help you out,' she said.

Everyone looked up. Bridget rolled her eyes and waved her hand, as if to flip away all our attention.

'No big deal,' she said. 'I can see how much Ash wants to do this hip hop stuff. We get discount class passes at the store, so you can use those.'

Bridget works at the Danceworks store in Somersby. She doesn't really dance, but when she got fired from the bakery and needed some work, Brimax got her the job because he knows the manager.

'Really, Bridge?' I asked.

'Yeah, don't worry about it,' she said. 'Maybe you can help out around the store or even at Silver Shoes to cover the rest. Why don't you ask Miss Caroline if there's something you can do at the studios?'

'I can do that,' I said.

'I hope this is all worth it,' grumbled Dad.

'Of course it is,' said Bridget. 'It means a lot to Ash.' She gave me a smile. 'Now finish your pasta, it's getting cold.'

'Yeah dig in, Ash,' joked Dad. 'Your mum didn't even use a packet this time.'

'Thank you so much,' I said, grinning at Bridget.

Dad forked his pasta in and Mum stared down at her food like she'd lost her appetite.

But I cannot tell you how excited I was. I would have swept a hundred floors if it meant I could do hip hop.

I just hoped Miss Caroline would agree.

Chapter Five

Miss Caroline did agree!

She said I could do the hip hop classes
with the discount passes. To make up the rest,
she said I could clean, tidy and organise the
costume and props rooms for half an hour
before or after my three classes a week.

'They are such a mess, I've been meaning
to get them sorted for ages,' she said. 'After
you've done those we can look at something

else for you to do. Although going by the state of the rooms, that will probably take you until you're old and grey.'

'You're the best!' I said.

Miss Caroline winked at me. 'What's say we keep our little arrangement just between you and me,' she said. 'For now.'

That suited me just fine, I didn't really want Jasmine and Tove on my back about being the hired help at Silver Shoes. I didn't even care about sorting out the dusty costume and props rooms. It actually sounded fun!

'Hi Tove,' I sang as I walked past her in the change room.

Tove shot me a glare that could rival the wicked witch. Whoa. I suddenly saw why Ellie sometimes compared her to a meerkat. 'Do not tell *anyone* I was at hip hop,' she said.

'What?' I said. 'Oh. Okay. Why? You looked like you were really having fun.'

'Be quiet, Ashley,' said Tove. 'Just please don't say anything.'

'If you're going to keep doing the class, people will find out soon enough,' I said.

Jasmine walked up then and hooked her arm through Tove's. Her pointy, pretty face looked extra haughty today. I think her eyebrows had been raised by two centimetres. 'Hey Tovey,' she said. 'Nice tights,' she added to me.

Typical Jasmine-ism. She said that because it's painfully obvious my tights are not nice. They're the wrong colour and have a big rip up the side, which Bridget mended. The only reason I have them at all is because they were in the discount basket at Danceworks and Bridget nicked them for me because they're purple, and that's my favourite colour.

'Nice wig,' I said back to her. 'Oh, sorry, that's your hair.'

Then I walked away. That's a really good trick. Always leave before they have a chance to say something back. That way, you'll always win.

'Hey Ash,' said Riley. She was already in class, sprawled out on the floor, one long leg propped up against the other. Her tight black curls were scraped into a sideways braid and she'd threaded a red ribbon through them.

'Heya Riley Cyrus,' I said. 'What happened?' There was a bandage around her middle finger and gauze wrapped around her hand.

'Hurt it at basketball,' she said. 'No big deal.'

'Should you be dancing?' I asked.

'Probably not.' She shrugged. 'Who cares? It's fine.' Her eyes took on the 'Riley' look, where they kind of slide over you and fix blankly on the first available sight. It's her way of saying 'the conversation is closed'.

Ellie flounced over then, and dropped down next to us, singing some musical theatre song. Musical theatre is her new style. She's obsessed. Her voice broke on the last note.

'That was nice,' said Riley. The corner of her mouth twitched up as she bit back her laugh.

'I haven't warmed up,' said Ellie. She was wearing a bright pink leotard with shiny silver stars. Anyone else would get in trouble because in technique class you're meant to wear a plain neutral leotard. But Ellie gets away with stuff like that.

'How was the hip hop class?' asked Riley.

'What hip hop class?' Ellie's head snapped up.

'I took a trial hip hop class the other day,' I said.

Ellie's face went a little dark. Her big green eyes stared me down and I could see the cogs working in her brain. *Will this hip hop class*

make her a better dancer than me? Will it give her an edge?

Ellie and I are friends, but sometimes she can still be a bit iffy around me – like any moment I'll reveal I actually am a Dance Art spy. I guess it's New Girl syndrome.

'Oh,' she said. 'Cool. Anyone we know in it?'

'Serah,' I said. I looked over at Tove. 'I think that's it.'

'Was it fun?' Riley asked.

'Amazing,' I said. 'I'm going to start taking the classes!'

'No way!' Ellie sat back. 'Really?'

'Yep,' I said.

'Are you going to start wearing high tops and backwards baseball caps too?' joked Riley.

'Of course,' I said. 'And jeans belted below my bum.'

'You shouldn't make fun of your own dance style,' said Ellie. 'If it *is* going to be your new style.'

'It is,' I said. 'I really love it.'

Ellie picked at the shiny silver stars on her leotard. 'Well, I'm going to try out for that Danceworks competition to be the face of the new hip hop dancewear range.'

'But you don't take hip hop,' Riley said.

'That shouldn't matter,' said Ellie. 'The poster for it said they want real dancers. I'm a real dancer.'

'It also said, "Do you hip hop? Are you ready to bring out your best moves?"'

'Well, Riley,' said Ellie, hands on her hips, 'it also said, "Do you want to represent your dance school by being the face of Freestyle?" And I've been at Silver Shoes longer than anyone, and I'm one of the best dancers, so really I think I have more right to try out than, say, some new girl who's come from another school and done one hip hop class.'

Gee, I wonder who she could have meant?

Riley gave me a sideways glance.

There was silence.

Luckily Paige tiptoed daintily into class at that moment. She looked embarrassed and out of breath. 'Hi,' she whispered to all of us, pushing wisps of hair off her face. 'Whoops. Just made it.'

For the next hour we learnt various ways to point our feet and stretch our bodies into positions that would rival a rubber man. Then we were shown how to jump, leap, transition, travel, run, turn and hold our backs correctly. Then we worked on tricks.

All the while I was thinking about the Danceworks competition.

I realised I really wanted to enter.

But the question was, should I tell Ellie or not?

Chapter Six

Sweetheart camisoles, halter leotards, character skirts, wrap skirts, racer back crop tops, ribbed singlets, booties, striped capris, knitted shrugs, dance sneakers, dance boots, feet gumbies, dance paws . . .

Going into a dance store is like entering heaven. The best ones smell like backstage – new tights, hairspray, make-up and fresh cotton. This one did. There were so many colours and styles of dance clothes, and then shelves of dance bags, shoes and drink bottles. And that wasn't counting the accessory displays – hairnets, ribbons, tape, make-up and ten styles of bobby pins.

I was at the Danceworks store, waiting for Bridget to finish her shift. I'd walked all the way from school. It was stinking hot, and my squished toes were losing the battle with my hand-me-down shoes. My backpack felt like a tonne of bricks on my sweaty back.

'Bridge won't be long, babe,' called out Stacey, who works at the front desk. She has the sharpest nails and the longest eyelashes I've ever seen. 'She's just finishing off the labels on the new stock.' Stacey was lounging on the front counter, so I didn't see why she couldn't pop into the back room and help Bridget out.

'That's cool,' I said, hoisting my backpack up.

'Hey, you want a drink bottle or something?' Stacey swung around and heaved a cardboard box up onto the shelf. 'We've got all these drink bottles to give away. You want one? There's pink, or purple, or you like blue? We got blue. Yeah? You want one?'

'Sure,' I said. The pink one was an Ellie shade of pink. I chose purple.

'Just be careful when you drink, cool? Sometimes the water leaks out when you tip it up. I think that's why we're giving them away for free. Hi there, how you going?'

I opened my mouth to reply, when I realised the store door had just opened and Stacey wasn't talking to me.

She was talking to two girls.

Two girls and one of their mums.

The last three people on earth I wanted to see.

I turned away and pretended to be really interested in the rows of bobby pins near the front counter. For the record, bobby pins aren't interesting. And they have a habit of getting lost after you wear them once.

But the two girls were Indianna and Daisy – two girls from my old school, Dance Art. Two girls who'd once put fish heads in my dance bag while I was in class.

Yeah, I guess you could say we'd never been friends.

'You need help with anything?' Stacey trilled.

'Tights!' Indianna's mum declared. 'Tights, tights, tights!'

Stacey went to show them the tights and I snuck back out into the hot afternoon sun. I found my water bottle and had a drink, but there was only a trickle left. Just when I was debating whether to go find a tap to fill up my new purple bottle, I heard the door swing open behind me.

Then came the witches' cackle.

'Nice drink bottle,' said Indianna. 'That's about the only thing you'll ever get from Danceworks. I thought you did all your shopping at Savers.'

'Only my earplugs,' I said. 'And you're right; they don't work well, because I can still hear you.'

'Real funny,' said Daisy.

'Thank you,' I said.

'So we heard you were at Silver Shoes now,' said Indianna.

'Poor you,' said Daisy.

'Well, you didn't hear it,' I said. 'You *saw* me at the Jazz Groove competition a few weeks ago. That's okay, not all of us know the difference between eyes and ears. Oh yeah, that was the competition you swore you'd never go to. And let me just think about this . . . that's right, Silver Shoes won. My new studio.'

Daisy and Indianna both huffed and rolled their eyes. Indianna tossed her glossy brown curls and, on cue, Daisy tossed her two long shiny black pigtails. Both their faces went into identical sniffy expressions. I swear they'd practised in the mirror.

'Whatever,' said Daisy. 'That comp is so dumb we weren't even trying.'

'Why bother turning up at all?' I said.

'For a laugh,' said Indianna.

'You don't need to go to a comp to have people laugh at you,' I said. 'They'll do it for free.'

'Tove told us you were doing hip hop now,' sniffed Daisy. 'At least that's more in line with the kind of clothes you wear.'

'Money doesn't buy taste,' I said, but I could feel the throat bubble again. I was hungry and hot, my backpack was heavy, and the only reason Daisy and Indianna had come out of the shop at all was because there were two of them.

I was sick of being teased about money and my clothes and being the girl who left Dance Art to be the new girl at Silver Shoes. None of that meant I couldn't dance well, or I didn't have a right to do what all the other girls did.

I swallowed the bubble. I held up my head. I marched over to the tap and I turned it on as much as it would go. The water hit the hot cement and splashed onto Indianna and Daisy.

'Gross!' they shrieked, leaping away.

'Whoops,' I said.

While I was filling up my bottle someone jogged up behind me. 'Hey Ash,' Brimax said, ruffling my hair. 'What's up?'

'Just came out here for the entertainment,' I said, looking over at Daisy and Indianna, who were dancing around trying to flick the water off.

'Slow day then,' said Brimax, with his crooked smirk. 'Hi girls.'

'Hi,' they mumbled.

'Looking nice and cool,' Brimax said cheerfully. He had all his muscles on display in his low-cut singlet and there was some new symbol shaved into the side of his cropped hair. Brimax thinks he's tough, but he's really a total goofball.

'What are you doing here?' I asked.

'Picking up Bridget,' he said. 'She about finished?'

'I think so. Just doing labels or something.'

'Sick,' said Brimax. He picked me up and tucked me under his arm. 'Let's go rescue her. I'm hungry and we three have a pizza date. See you later, girls.'

Yeah, see you later, I thought. *See you when I'm the new face of the Danceworks hip hop range.*

Because now I was even more determined than ever.

Chapter Seven

Aaaaa-chooooo!

It sure was dusty in the Silver Shoes costume room.

When I first walked in, I saw the costumes from the latest performance all hanging up neatly on the racks. And a desk with the bibs and bobs you need to put the finishing touches on any costume – needles, cotton, sequins, safety pins, velcro straps.

But beyond that.

Wow.

I'm talking chests and cartons overflowing with material, piles of mismatched shoes, unfinished versions of costumes and bundles of hats, gloves, skirts and headpieces.

There was some great stuff there. If I ever needed to go to a costume party, I was in the right place.

I decided it was best to just jump right in with my first attempt at tidying and sorting out this Silver Shoes mess.

I moved the neat racks into the props room, and then shoved everything as best as I could onto one side of the floor. Then I dashed off to the storage room to find some tubs to begin my sorting.

Each tub had a label: Junk – throw out, Hats, Accessories, Full sets, Could be used again, Material scraps. But as I began my sorting I realised I was making another little pile next to me: the Ashley pile.

Because I was beginning to get ideas about the Danceworks photo shoot.

While I was sussing out some lace, trying to decide if it was too yellow to be used, there was a knock on the costume room door, which I'd left open.

'Hey Ash,' said Riley. 'What are you doing?'

'Oh,' I said. 'Um. Just hanging with the costumes. Get it, hanging?'

Riley giggled. 'Better luck next time.'

'Must be all this dust clogging my funny veins,' I said. 'Well, actually . . .' I paused, wondering if I should tell Riley the truth. She might be angry that I was getting a special deal. But then I knew I couldn't lie. Riley was my best friend at Silver Shoes.

'Miss Caroline said if I helped around Silver Shoes I could pay for part of my hip hop lessons that way,' I said. 'Because Mum and Dad don't really have that extra money at the moment.'

I paused again, waiting to see what she'd say.

But Riley just shrugged. 'Cool,' she said. 'That's a smart idea.' She peered around the corner of the door and made a face. 'Looks like you got the bad end of the deal, though. What a mess!' She pointed at an old scarecrow costume. 'I remember that! That was for our Under 7s jazz eisteddfod – *The Wizard of Oz*. Paige was Dorothy and Jasmine was the wicked witch.'

'Sounds about right,' I said.

Riley laughed. 'Jasmine really suited the part.' She pointed at the little pile next to me. 'What's that?'

'Well,' I said, 'I was thinking, if it's okay with Miss Caroline, that I could use them for the Danceworks competition. I'm going to enter.'

'Good!' said Riley, sitting down next to me. 'I hoped you would.'

'You know how to enter you have to send in some modelling pictures of yourself and a page about why you love hip hop?'

'Yeah,' said Riley.

'Well, I was thinking, because I don't have any proper shots already, or, you know, like the latest hip hop clothes or whatever, that it might be cool if I sent in photos of me dressed up in costumes that show hip hop style throughout the years. Influences, stuff like that. I've been watching a lot of hip hop history on YouTube, so I'm collecting anything that I think might work for the photos.'

'Ash, that's an excellent idea!' said Riley. 'No one else will think of that. Can I help? With the photos? My dad's got a really good camera I can ask to borrow.'

'Yeah sure,' I said. 'I want to ask the other girls as well, but I know that Ellie wants to enter the comp too, so it might be a bit weird. And Paige will probably want to help her.'

'You can only ask,' Riley said. 'But this will totally catch their eye. So exciting!' She pushed me into the dusty, smelly pile of costumes. 'Just remember me when you're famous!'

'Never,' I said, pushing her back. 'Who are you again?'

'What!' Riley laughed. She swung some mouldy velvet at me. 'Maybe this will make you remember!'

And that's how the costume room ended up looking worse than when I began.

Chapter Eight

The night before my first paying hip hop class, Brimax and Bridget took me to a fund-raising hip hop gig that Brimax's crew was putting on.

'There's a hip hop festival for kids in about a month,' Brimax said. 'My crew are organising it. Tonight is a sneak preview of all the good stuff to come – we're having a battle showdown and the money raised will go towards the festival.'

At first Bridget turned her nose up and said it wasn't suitable for me to watch, but then Brimax and I teamed up and won her over.

'It's in the name of research,' I said.

'Yeah, for Ash's great hip hop career to come,' added Brimax.

'You two are as bad as each other,' she said, but I could tell she was trying not to smile.

The fundraising battle was so cool. It was just like what I'd seen in some of my favourite dancing movies (which I watched without telling Mum because she didn't think they were 'appropriate').

The showdown was in this community hall and there was a big space in the middle for the dancing. People were sitting around it or handing out flyers for the upcoming festival. The lights were all hazy and there was a remix of hip hop beats playing.

Brimax walked in, clapping people's backs and being everyone's best friend. Bridget stood off to one side, clinging onto my arm. She looked unimpressed.

While Brimax went off to warm up with his crew, Bridget and I sat on some blocks near the wall because Bridget didn't want to be crushed by 'smelly armpits and gold chains'.

It didn't smell that bad. But Bridget's fussy like that. She spends two hours getting ready every morning, maybe three if she knows she's going to see Brimax. Besides, she was trying to fit in really bad, I could tell. Her ash-blonde hair was covered by a beanie and she was wearing jeans instead of one of her usual girly dresses.

The battle started. Brimax had managed to get about eight crews to take part. Some were huge and others only had three or four people. First, each crew performed their dance and then the crowd had to vote on which crews they wanted to battle. Whoever won would go on to the next round.

I was itching to get up and dance myself, but Bridget kept a stern eye on me. She only relaxed when Brimax danced. Then she went all melty and goggle-eyed.

I loved watching the girls; they were outnumbered a bit by the boys but they made up for it in attitude. A lot of them had these really outrageous hairstyles and some of the funkiest high tops I've ever seen.

The best thing about the costumes was that they weren't just something a teacher had knocked together. They were expressions of each person. I liked that. I stored away some ideas for my hip hop shoot.

In the end, a crew called 'Reggae Fusion' got voted as the winners. Their style was dancehall, full of Jamaican flavour. The crew weren't big on tricks but they were smooth and so in sync. Sometimes it looked like their bodies had no bones. Jay would have called them 'tight'.

That night my body was buzzing and I could barely sleep, I was so excited about my hip hop class the next day.

Jay didn't disappoint.

'And we go pop, lock, hold it, glide, heel, toe, kick, walk-it-out, knee, drop, turn and hold,' he shouted. My feet got so tangled it felt like the only flat I would be doing was on my face. 'Body roll front,' he shouted next. 'And we go floor sweep right, floor sweep left.'

A floor sweep is where you kind of sweep the floor in a circular motion with your foot and then move backwards on the other one. It sounds easy, but then you have to put the groove into it. Every time I tried to do that, things got a bit unco.

Then we did this locking sequence that reminded me of Michael Jackson when he danced, all these movements with bent knees and small freezes for emphasis. Your arms and hands are in constant motion, like you're trying to hit the beats as they come out of your feet.

It was HARD work. At times I got totally lost and had to stop, but I always picked it back up.

'How you going, Ashy?' asked Jay.

'Loving it,' I said. 'My feet get a bit confused, though. All these moves I haven't heard of before.'

'You're doing great for your second lesson,' Jay said. 'And you know what? You're thinking too much about it, I bet. Just go with the beat. Enjoy.'

'But I want to be good,' I said.

'You are,' said Jay.

'I want to be better,' I said.

'Now you sound like Ellie.' Jay grinned.

'I'm not wearing enough pink,' I joked.

'There!' said Jay, pointing at my face. 'That's what I need to see more of. It doesn't matter if you don't know everything technical or the right name for the move. You've only had two lessons. You'll pick it up. All you need to do is get the feel of the music. Listen to your body. If your arm goes left instead of right, who cares?' He slung his baseball cap on my head. 'Except, of course, if you're in a competition. Then we get serious.'

'Your cap stinks like sweaty hair,' I said.

'Well, you got the 'tude, all right.' Jay laughed.

He let me keep his baseball cap until the end of the lesson. I don't know if it was a good luck charm or what, but I did relax, and I stopped listening to him calling out the names of moves and turned my attention to the music instead.

Jazz class was on Wednesday, and although it was now my second favourite style, I was so excited to see Ellie, Riley and Paige, and to fill them in on this new style I couldn't get out of my head.

We met up in the change room and were just sharing a big packet of jelly snakes (usually one of us will bring snakes every lesson), when we all heard a voice behind us.

Our worst nightmare.

Chapter Nine

'*This* is your dressing room? Ugh. It looks like where someone would go to die.'

Indianna and Daisy! Spies from Dance Art. At *our* school! And even worse, Jasmine and Tove were trailing behind them. They'd actually let the enemy in!

'What are *they* doing here?' Riley said.

'Oh,' said Jasmine. 'Hi.'

'Bye,' said Riley.

'Not only is this school poor, it's also unfriendly,' sniffed Indianna. Her lips looked extra pouty today.

'What are you doing here?' asked Ellie again.

'Jasmine's mum ran us home from school,' said Daisy. 'We're waiting to get picked up.'

'Wait outside,' said Riley.

'We don't want spies in here,' added Ellie.

'Too late,' said Indianna, looking at me. 'Oh, hi again, Ashley. Where's your protector this time?'

'Waiting with the hose,' I said. 'You look like you need cooling down again.'

'As if we came in here to spy,' said Daisy. 'Like there's anything to steal around here. It's an old church.'

Silver Shoes is in an old church, but it isn't as bad as Daisy suggests. It was a huge church to begin with, and it's been renovated, with mirrors and new shiny wood.

It's also divided into three different studios: two main ones in the church and a smaller one in the old hall out the back. There are lots of long corridors that seem to lead nowhere. Even though it's kind of kiddie, Paige and I have often played hide-and-seek in the dark rooms and shadowy hallways.

'Maybe it wasn't a good idea to let them in, Jasmine,' said Paige. 'I'm not sure Miss Caroline would like it. We do go up against them at comps and stuff.'

Jasmine sighed. Out of all of us, she probably likes Paige the best. That's because Paige is rich, and so is Jasmine. Their mums hate each other, though, which they both find embarrassing, so they have this uneasy truce.

But Jasmine had her minions today. Jasmine, Tove, Indianna and Daisy go to the same rich girls' school. And so that meant bad news for Paige.

'How's your boyfriend, Paige?' asked Jasmine. She twirled her long caramel ponytail and looked out slyly from the corner of her eyes.

Paige went beet-red. 'What?'

'Didn't I see you dancing with some boy the other day?'

'He isn't her boyfriend, he's her dance partner,' said Ellie. The freckles across her nose were standing out; it always happens when she gets angry. 'Duh. Some of us want to try new styles to better ourselves. Others are just happy with the same old stuff.' She made a point of looking at all four of them. 'Whether they're good or not.'

'Guess that's why at the last comp I beat you,' said Jasmine.

'Where's that grace dancers are meant to carry themselves with?' I said.

'What class are you all about to do, anyway?' asked Indianna. 'Jazz, just boring old jazz? Not all these new styles you're trying to do? Hip hop?' She blinked her long lashes at Ellie. 'Musical theatre? Ballroom?' This one was to Paige. Then she looked at Riley. 'Whatever you do.'

'State athletics team, long jump, triple jump, and two-hundred-metre champion,' said Riley. 'But you should know. Weren't you at the inter-schools athletics carnival this year? You know, you were the team that dropped the baton in the relay? If I remember right.'

Indianna seemed shocked but then she looked at her minions and made a quick recovery. 'Like I care about some relay,' she said. 'I go to Dance Art Academy. I'm going to be a famous dancer.'

'Don't see why you're hanging around here then,' said Riley.

'I just thought that was normal,' said Indianna. 'I mean, look at Ashley. She started hanging around here. Why was that again? Oh. Because she couldn't afford to stay at Dance Art.'

'It's none of your business why she did or didn't leave,' said Paige. 'And we love having her here anyway.'

'Why? Because she makes you all look good?'

'Or because she thinks she's going to be the new face of the Danceworks dance range?' sniffed Jasmine.

Gosh. There are no secrets in dance school! Jasmine must have had her spies out to learn I was going to enter the competition. I hadn't even told Ellie yet!

'Why would they pick anyone like you?' said Indianna. 'They're not going to choose some school-swapper. Or someone who can't even dance.'

'You're very hung up on the fact that Ashley left Dance Art,' said Riley. 'Probably jealous. Why else would you be here now? I think you're the spy, and you're trying to find out what it is that makes Silver Shoes so much better than Dance Art.'

'Ugh,' said Daisy. 'We've got better things to do.'

'So have we,' said Riley. 'Now, if you'll excuse us, I think we've breathed enough germs for one day.' She shut the dressing room door in their faces.

'I hope they're gone when we go out to class,' said Paige.

'Jasmine's gonna get in so much trouble from Miss Caroline for bringing them inside,' said Ellie, gleefully.

'It's sad if they've got nothing better to do than to come in here and be all snotty,' said Riley.

'Are you really entering the Danceworks competition?' Ellie asked me.

'Yep,' I said. 'Sorry. I know you want to, as well.' Ellie was quiet for a moment. It was like watching a volcano – would she erupt or just simmer along quietly? I felt like our friendship was hanging off what she'd say next.

'Oh well, good luck, I guess,' she finally said. But she didn't look at me.

'Well, Ash,' said Riley, jumping in, 'you're lucky you did come to Silver Shoes. Imagine if you'd stayed at Dance Art. You'd turn out like *them*.'

'Oh, the horror,' I joked.

'Have a snake,' said Paige, holding out the packet. 'You can pretend it's Indianna and Daisy's heads.'

I grabbed two and took a big bite. Snakes never tasted so good! But when I became the best hip hop dancer ever, and the face of the Danceworks Freestyle range, I knew it would taste even better.

Chapter Ten

All week I'd been watching hip hop videos on YouTube, to the point where Bridget got angry at me because she said I was using up all the download limit.

'Sorry,' I said, but when she was cooking dinner, I got Brimax to help me with a playlist of the 'best hip hop songs ever'.

'These are the must-haves,' he said proudly, handing me the iPod. 'And so begins your education.'

I turned the iPod on and jammed along to all my new songs while I was cleaning out the costume room at Silver Shoes. It was shaping up well, and I was getting a nice little pile of outfits for my shoot. On top of that, I couldn't believe I was up to my third hip hop class already!

Jay made us stretch a lot. It wasn't like jazz, though, where you spend a lot of time doing one stretch, and you switch cleanly from one to the other. Jay's style was really fluid. It reminded me of yoga, which I'd seen Bridget doing in her bedroom (when she thought no one was watching).

''Cause we gotta get limber,' Jay said, as we did side lunges, bam, bam, bam, left to right with barely a pause. Then we did ten minutes just on abs. I was used to that, because we did a lot of core work in jazz, but my abs were grumbling at me by the end.

I looked over at Tove, and she pulled a face like she felt my pain. It made me laugh, which made my abs hurt more.

As soon as we got up to dance, my shoe decided to fall apart. The whole sole of my left Chucks began to peel away, and a big split appeared on the side. I tried to keep dancing with it, but Jay's eyes were as sharp as his moves.

'Lose the shoes, Ash,' he said to me while the others were getting a drink. 'You look like a seagull flapping about.'

Of course once the shoes were gone and I got over the embarrassment of being barefoot (no one noticed anyway), I found myself hitting everything that Jay showed us. I was getting familiar with my own hip hop style and the moves came out the way my body told them to, instead of me trying to mimic everyone else.

There was even partner work in the sequence that Jay taught us.

Guess who my partner was.

Guess.

Tove.

I thought she would drop me, because she had to catch my hands and help flip me over so I did a mini somersault in the air. Then we both did a front aerial.

It sounded scary but we practised on the mats first, and having someone else's hands supporting me and holding me up meant it was unlikely I'd go splat on the floor.

Plus I'd done gymnastics for a few years when I was younger, so I was pretty good at tricks or anything acro.

Tove and I kept hitting it, over and over again, and eventually Tove was flipping me over so fast and we were doing our aerials in

sync that Jay started hollering, 'Look at Cirque du Soleil over here!'

You know what? I started to feel like Tove and I could be friends. I guess having someone stop you from face-planting into the floor makes you start liking them a bit.

Jay called us over after class. 'Girls, girls!' he said. 'Killing it! Those flips! You come straight from the Olympics or what?'

'I'm an undercover gymnast,' I said.

'I'm just naturally good,' said Tove, but she was joking. Who knew she had a sense of humour hidden under that Jasmine-inspired scowl!

'So I've got a proposition for you,' said Jay.

'A what?' said Tove.

'I wanna make you an offer,' Jay said.

'Ten million bucks,' I said.

'Keep dreaming,' said Jay. 'I'll give you ten dollars.'

'This better be good then,' I joked.

'You'll love it!' said Jay. 'Listen up. There's a hip hop festival coming up in about a month.'

'I know!' I said. 'I went to the fundraiser night for it. It looks awesome!'

'Look at you, all down with the battles,' said Jay.

'I'm G,' I said, which was something I'd heard them say in one of the dance movies I'd watched.

Jay laughed. 'You're not G, but you both know how to hit it. So I want you to be in the junior crew I'm putting together. I got asked to choreograph something for the final showcase. You in?'

'I'll have to ask my mum,' said Tove, 'but I think it will be fine.'

'We'll be rehearsing the Sundays leading up to it,' Jay said. 'Maybe extra if we need to.'

'Is there a cost involved?' I asked.

'Nah,' said Jay. 'You just gotta turn up and show me what you got.'

'Okay,' I said, 'sounds good.'

'Good?' said Jay.

'It sounds exciting!' I said.

'I'll ask my mum and let you know tomorrow when I'm here for jazz. Will you be around?' asked Tove.

'I'm always around,' said Jay. 'Miss Caroline won't let me leave.'

'Cool,' said Tove. 'See ya then.'

'See ya,' said Jay to her flying braids as she ran out the door. He turned to me. 'You in, AshFunK?'

'Definitely,' I said.

'That's the way,' said Jay. 'But, Ash? You gotta get some new kicks.'

'Kicks?'

'Shoes,' said Jay. 'You gotta work some funky high tops.' He pointed at my torn, dirty

Chucks in the corner. 'I think they've danced their last step. Those babies are done.'

'No problem,' I said. 'I'll see what I can come up with.'

I knew what I would come up with. Nothing. Or a pair of Bridget's old, dirty netball sneakers.

Unless, of course, I won the Danceworks comp.

But I'd deal with that later. Because:

I had a crew!

I was going to dance in a hip hop competition!

A lack of shoes wasn't going to hold me back!

Chapter Eleven

The community centre looked like an elephant had trodden on it and there was faded graffiti all over the walls.

'Nice place,' Tove said, grimacing.

'Guess we'll soon find out,' I said.

Inside, it smelled like disinfectant and the corner of our garage where the rain leaked onto the old carpet.

'You here for the hip hop rehearsal?' asked a

boy, appearing round the corner of a hallway that led off into dark, smelly depths.

'Uhhhh . . . yes?' said Tove. She was totally out of her element.

'Cool, down here,' said the boy. He opened a door to our right.

I watched as he walked ahead of us. 'Do I know you from somewhere?' I asked.

He flicked his eyes at me but kept walking. 'Don't think so,' he said. 'Come on.'

There were some steps that led down into a basement space. The walls were draped with curtains and there were milk crates everywhere, and movable flats. They had reflective vinyl sheets on them so they looked like mirrors.

Apart from the boy, there were about ten other kids, mostly around our age.

I quickly looked around. Phew. Some of the kids weren't wearing shoes. I wouldn't be either, because, well, I didn't have any. I was just going to use the excuse that I forgot, but I thought that if some of the others weren't wearing shoes, maybe it wouldn't matter.

At least until the performance. But hopefully I'd be rolling in my own Danceworks Freestyle hip hop range by then.

When everyone was inside, sitting around on the crates, Jay did his thing.

'Welcome to my palace,' he said. 'Thank you for coming!'

It was a bit weird to see him outside of the Silver Shoes studios, even though he was still teaching us dance, like normal. He looked too clean and proper to be hanging out in a basement, although his friendly eyes and super smile were still the same.

'This is my boy Ryan,' Jay clapped hands with a tall guy next to him, who I think I'd seen at the fundraiser event. 'We're gonna put together the best dance ever for this festival. We're closing the show, it's gonna be tight, it's gonna be crazy, it's gonna be fun! Who's ready?'

Everyone cheered, except Tove, who kind of squeaked.

The song Jay had picked was called 'Son of a Gun' by Janet Jackson and Missy Elliott. It was this really funky remix where all the girls were meant to be rich and the boys broke into our mansion to steal our money, except then we girls turned into monsters and scared them off.

There were all these cool hand clap rhythms, which Jay told us was our chance to 'really hit it', and the song had a soft, constant drumbeat that set the pace.

It was quite scary-sounding and there were lots of creepy sound effects like tap drips and echoes and electric guitar riffs. 'Use all these sounds to get into monster mode,' Jay told us. 'Own the sounds, the creepiness.'

It was crazy fun. The dance was a softer style of hip hop with lots of pauses for effect. Sometimes it even seemed a little contemporary with strange body shapes and stilted movements.

Tove was really funny when she first tried to be a monster.

'You look like a chicken coming out of its egg, not a zombie lady who wants revenge,' I said.

'I'm so embarrassed,' said Tove. 'How do I act all dead and angry? I've never been dead before.'

'Just think of how you feel when Miss Caroline makes us go over a dance for the hundredth time because *one* person is behind the beat,' I said.

Jay taught us the whole dance in the first

rehearsal, except for a sequence at the end. It wasn't as tough as it had sounded because there were sections where the boys danced for 32 counts while we were offstage, and then we came on and danced for 32 while they had to pretend to be scared and hide.

There was also partner work towards the end. I was put with the boy we'd met at the start. His name was Benji.

At first I felt a bit shy but he was a really good partner, even if sometimes his back was kinda stiff – unlike poor Tove who kept bumping into her partner and scowling at him.

'You're really good!' said Benji. 'Where do you dance?'

'At Silver Shoes,' I said.

'Oh yeah, I know someone from there,' he said.

'Who?' I said.

He went a bit pink. 'Never mind,' he said.

'Do you dance other styles?' I asked, trying to make him feel comfortable.

Benji went pinker. 'Oh yeah, a few,' he said. 'Hey, you wanna go over that last eight count?'

I knew well enough when someone doesn't want to talk.

'Sure,' I said.

When we'd finished rehearsing I was exhausted! The ground wasn't sprung floorboards like at Silver Shoes and my bare feet didn't exactly provide a lot of padding.

But still, I felt right at home, and I knew if I wanted to keep the feeling going, there was one thing I really had to do:

I had to ask Mum about new shoes.

Chapter Twelve

Mum was in the kitchen, chopping up carrots. I say chopping, but she was more hacking at them while reading something written in a notebook.

'You'll chop off your finger,' I said.

'Hmm?' she said.

'You'll cut your finger,' I said.

'Oh,' said Mum. 'Bit of extra flavour. I'm doing a roast. Aunty Liz gave me this cut of lamb. The butcher gave her extra.'

'Did you have a good day?' I asked, picking up a potato and cutting it into cubes. Mum and Dad like them cut in half but there's this special spice Bridget puts on the potatoes and it tastes better when they're in cubes.

'What? Oh it was okay. Busy. Be careful with that knife.'

'It's nice you're making dinner,' I said.

Mum looked up for a second. 'Yes, well, I feel a bit bad sometimes, leaving you girls to fend for yourselves. It will be lovely to have a good family meal.'

Bridget came in then.

'You'll cut your finger,' she said to Mum, who was still mutilating the carrots.

'Oh stop fussing,' said Mum. 'Did you have a good day? Not seeing Brimax tonight?'

'He's at some hip hop thing,' Bridget said. 'That's all he goes on about lately. Seems to be in the air.' She gave me a wink.

Mum tipped the carrots into a bowl and dragged over some pumpkin. 'That's nice,' she said. 'Shall I take the skin off or leave it on?'

'Off,' said Bridget.

'Ash is becoming a real little hip hopper, or so I heard,' said Bridget.

'Yes, I've been meaning to ask,' said Mum. 'How are you going with it, Ashy?'

'It's so much fun, Mum,' I said. 'I'm going to be in a hip hop festival in a few weeks!'

'Didn't take you long,' said Mum, looking up and smiling at me.

'Do you want to come and watch?' I asked.

Then I wanted to take it back. Mum and Dad hardly ever see me dance. They're always working. I know they kind of have to, but sometimes when I see Paige's mum fussing over her and Riley's parents cheering and waving in the audience, I get a bit sad.

I guess I'm a pretty good dancer and it would be nice for them to see that, and to see how much I love dancing. I always tell them it's fine that they can't come. But I know they would go if I said I really wanted them there.

'When is it?' said Mum, cutting the skin off the pumpkin, and half the pumpkin with it.

'It's in a few Sundays time,' I said. 'In the evening.'

'Sure,' said Mum. 'If I'm not doing the Sunday shift at the club. It's very busy on Sundays.'

'I'll be there,' said Bridget, taking the potato cubes and dumping them into the bowl with a little more force than she probably needed to. 'I wouldn't miss it for the world, Ash.'

'There's one other thing.'

'Hmm?'

I poked at the carrot and potato. 'I need

some new shoes for it,' I said.

Mum frowned. 'Why?'

'The sole came off my old ones,' I said. 'Jay is doing all the costumes for the performance but I need these special high top shoes for it. Everyone has to have them. And I can keep using them in class afterwards.'

'How much are they?' Mum studied the pumpkin like it was still on the vine, growing before her eyes.

'Um,' I said. 'About a hundred bucks. For a good pair.'

'A hundred dollars?' said Mum. She began to cut the pumpkin again. 'I don't think so.'

'But I need them,' I said.

'Sure you do. Wear your sandshoes.'

'That won't win any cool awards,' I joked.

'I'm sorry, Ash, but that is out of our price range at the moment. You'll have to think of something else.'

Oh well. Worth a try. It was lucky I *did* have something else up my sleeve.

I had quite the collection now for my planned hip hop shoot. But I had to get onto it quickly because the closing date for submissions was next week!

The next time I was at Silver Shoes I did a final hunt around the costume and props rooms for anything I could use for the shoot. I was running out the door with a large armful when I crashed into someone.

Chapter Thirteen

'Oh, whoops!' I said, as my armful of clothes tumbled to the floor. 'Sorry!'

Then I realised who it was.

'What are you doing here?' I asked.

'Oh, hi, Ashley,' stuttered Benji. 'Um . . .'

'You never said you danced at Silver Shoes,' I said.

'Well, I don't, not really,' said Benji.

I looked at his clothes. And his sweaty face.

It *looked* like he'd been dancing.

'Just been running around the block then, have you?' I said.

Benji shifted his feet. He was wearing *very* dance-ish pointed shoes. They even had small heels.

'I like your high heels,' I said.

Benji scowled. 'They're *character* shoes,' he said, crossing his arms.

'If you say so,' I teased.

Benji's hair was also slicked back to the max. 'Your gel helmet is pretty cool, too,' I said. 'At least your head will be protected if you fall over.'

'It's for ballroom,' Benji snapped. 'I do ballroom classes. I don't *like* it. Mum makes me. Don't tell anyone at hip hop.'

'Oh,' I said, 'you're Paige's ballroom partner! I saw you rehearsing with her once.'

'We're dancing in a junior comp next week,' said Benji. 'That's what we were just practising for.'

'Paige didn't say she was in a comp,' I said.

'Well, she likes doing ballroom about as much as I do,' said Benji. He frowned. 'But that's because she does a million other classes.'

'Yeah, she doesn't talk about it much,' I said. 'Are you excited about the comp?'

'Ugh,' said Ben. 'It's all Mum's friends staring at me like vultures and swamping my head in hairspray. Like a whole bottle for one style. I hate that stuff. My hair isn't going to move. I don't even have that much of it!'

I laughed. 'I'd like to see that.'

'Come and watch if you want,' said Ben. 'If Paige doesn't mind. It'd be good to have some friendly faces there.' He started heading down the hall. 'See you at hip hop practice?'

'Wouldn't miss it,' I said.

Because of my chat with Benji, I was late for jazz class, and I was still half pulling on my tatty slippers when I entered the room. I lined up next to Riley, who had a huge bruise on her leg.

'Basketball,' she said, when she saw me looking at it. 'Don't be fooled by the name Saint Therese's Primary. They aren't saints.'

'Are you okay?' asked Paige, who'd caught the conversation.

'Are you?' I teased. Usually Paige looks like a doll, but today she looked like she'd been thrown around the room all afternoon by a toddler. She and Benji must have really been busting out the tango moves.

'I'm tired,' she confessed.

'I told you to have more lollies,' Ellie said, looking up from where she was stretching. 'I have that giant bag. If you don't eat them, Lucas will hunt them out and get hypo on too much sugar.' Lucas is Ellie's little brother. He's way cute.

'I heard you have a comp coming up,' I said to Paige. 'Next week.'

Paige brushed her blonde curls out of her eyes. 'How do you know that?' she asked.

'I ran into Benji,' I said.

'Ooooooh,' said Ellie. '*Benji.*'

'How do you know him?' asked Paige.

'He's in that hip hop thing I'm doing,' I said. 'You're lucky to have him as a partner. We dance together in the hip hop class and he's great. Really nice, too.'

'I bet he's nice when he's got two girls to choose from!' teased Riley.

'Yuck,' said Ellie. 'I'm not going to have any time for boys when I'm older. I'm going to be married to dance.'

'How did you run into him anyway?' asked Paige.

'I was getting some stuff from the costume room for the shoot and I bumped into him,' I said.

'I forgot about that!' said Paige. 'You're doing that tomorrow, right? Do you need some help?'

'Sure,' I said.

Silence. I could feel everyone trying not to look at Ellie. Paige did some stretches. Riley studied her bruise. I pretended to fix my fringe.

'Oh come on, guys,' Ellie finally said. 'It's fine. I'm not going to enter the competition anyway.'

I risked a look at her. I knew our friendship was already on thin ice. I really liked Ellie and I didn't want to ruffle any feathers.

'Really, it's fine,' Ellie said. 'It's stupid anyway. I don't need a new hip hop wardrobe, I don't even do hip hop. And, like, I'm so busy with my musical theatre stuff . . . and . . .' She sighed. 'Paige told me about your idea for the shoot, Ash. It sounds really fun. I'd like to help too. I can do your hair and make-up if you like.'

'I would love that,' I said.

'Cool,' said Ellie, and she went back to stretching as if she'd been on my side all along.

I was playing it cool, too, though. It meant a lot to me that Ellie wanted to help with the shoot.

It made me feel like I had really found my place at Silver Shoes.

It made me feel like I belonged.

Chapter Fourteen

'Careful of that camera!' Riley yelled. 'It's going to fall off the table and Dad will kill me!'

Paige rescued it and put it in the middle of a basket filled with scraps of material.

'Well, what do you expect?' said Ellie. 'I'm trying to do Ash's make-up, I need a lot of space.'

The desk in front of me was covered with lipsticks and glitter and eye pencils. We were in the costume room (which was starting to look very flash, I must say, after all my efforts), creating another look for my Danceworks shoot.

We'd done three shots, with five to go.

So far I'd been the Godfather of Soul, James Brown, and dressed in this crazy 70s costume with flared pants, a bright red billowy shirt and a vest. Riley took the shot of me on the stage in the community hall as I struck a pose behind the microphone.

Next I'd been Michael Jackson, in black pants, a white t-shirt and a sparkly glove, doing the moonwalk on the footpath out the front of Silver Shoes.

Then I'd dressed up as a member of the 90s hip hop girl band Salt-N-Pepa. I'd posed in front of the fence at the side of Silver Shoes. It was covered in graffiti. I'd found this crazy denim jacket with tight black lycra pants and a baseball cap, which we'd decorated with scraps from the costume room.

Now I was famous 90s rapper MC Hammer. I wore a sequinned crop-top vest and genie pants from an old *Aladdin* performance.

I'd pretty much got everything I needed from the costume room. Anything I didn't have, Ellie, Riley and Paige had brought. I guess they'd raided their parents' wardrobes.

We were getting a few weird looks as we raced around Silver Shoes, trying to find the best place to take the shots. But dressing up and posing for the photos was a blast. I really hoped it would be enough to win the Danceworks competition.

'I think you'll win for sure,' said Ellie, as she painted my lips in a dark maroon lipstick. 'I mean, you're really going all out. Everyone else will just send in, like, pretty modelling shots.'

'And you're showing that you know about the history of hip hop,' said Paige, winding a scrunchie around my high ponytail.

'Don't forget that you're using Silver Shoes to take all the shots,' said Riley. 'And it said on the advertisement that they want to get someone who is proud to represent their school and their style. What better way than this!'

'You're not too bad at this modelling thing either, Ash,' said Ellie.

'Been practising in the mirror,' I joked. 'Got all my best sides down pat.'

We went out into the hall to look for a place to do my next shot.

'How about there!' I said, pointing. 'In front of that stained-glass window? The light will look really good coming in from behind. And it goes with MC Hammer. He did a song called "Pray". I watched the video clip on YouTube.'

'I reckon for this one you should maybe do some moves and it can be like an action shot,' said Ellie.

'Oooh, you'll get to see some of what I've been learning,' I said. 'I should be charging for this!'

'A hairstylist, a make-up artist and a photographer?' said Ellie, pointing at herself, Riley and Paige. 'We should be charging *you*!'

'True.' I laughed. 'Seriously, though, thank you guys so much for helping me. It's way more fun than if I was doing it by myself.'

'That's what we're here for,' said Paige. 'Come on, we've got a Danceworks comp to win!'

I really hoped I did win. But even if I didn't, I was having the best time with my Silver Shoes friends.

That was worth far more than any new hip hop wardrobe.

Chapter Fifteen

For the next few weeks I kept going to my hip hop classes, and practising for the festival night. The more I did hip hop the more I loved it, and I was even starting to get the hang of a few simple breakdancing tricks!

My organisation of the costume room was going well, and when Miss Caroline peeked in one day she clapped her hands and said it looked fantastic.

'I'm really proud you took the initiative, Ashley,' she said to me. 'To work for what you want. It's very mature. I hope you're enjoying the hip hop classes. Jay has been singing your praises.'

'Well, it's helped me in more ways than one,' I said, thinking of how cleaning out the costume room had led to the photo shoot idea. 'Plus, it's kinda fun. I like being here at Silver Shoes.'

'And we like having you here,' said Miss Caroline.

'It's the least I can do,' I joked.

For the past few weeks I'd tried not to think too much about the Danceworks competition. I didn't want to get my hopes up. But I knew, in the back of my mind, I was waiting to hear from them.

Mainly because of one thing.

The festival night was coming up.

And I still didn't have any shoes.

I'd been going okay in my bare feet, but I couldn't go without shoes for the performance. It was part of the costume! My best idea was to 'borrow' a pair of Bridget's Skechers and stuff them with tissues so they wouldn't slip off.

So I would be wearing too-big, tissue-stuffed, girly Skechers, while everyone had awesome high tops. And I knew they were awesome, because everyone had been wearing them in practice.

Everyone except me.

***

I came home from school on Friday in a bad mood.

First, I'd walked home with a heavy back-pack because no one had picked me up.

Then, when I finally got in the front door, there was a message for me on the bench – 'Ash, can you please finish off the washing and put it out, thanks.' I hated hanging out the washing because I wasn't tall enough and the wet clothes always slapped me in the face and mussed up my hair.

When I went to the pantry to get some energy for this horrible chore, someone had eaten all the barbecue Shapes. *And put the empty packet back in the pantry!* So I didn't even have any snacks to look forward to.

Plus I was just tired from all the hip hop practice and my extra job at Silver Shoes, and I was worrying about the Danceworks comp.

Maybe the judges thought I'd been trying too hard. Or I was a bad model. Or I just didn't suit hip hop.

I stomped off to my room, yelling out rude things because I was the only one home and my toys had heard it all before.

Then I stopped.

There was a letter on my bed.

The label on the back said 'Danceworks'.

I took a big breath.

I tore open the envelope.

And I found out that I, Ashley Jenkyns, was going to be the new face of the Danceworks Freestyle hip hop range!

The letter said they loved my style, my attitude, and my originality. It also said that my love for hip hop had really shone through.

There was a date for when I should come and meet them and discuss the shoot.

But that wasn't the best bit.

The best bit was when I flicked through the catalogue of the hip hop wardrobe I'd won.

There was some cool stuff, of course. Some wicked t-shirts and crop tops, and a couple of pairs of hip hop dance pants that looked like they were straight out of a video clip.

But the coolest thing was, of course, the high tops.

My dream shoes.

It was just a picture, but I knew they'd be even better once they were on my feet. They were dark purple, with silver soles, gold embellishments and black laces.

But they weren't just any old high tops. They were dancing ones – the sole was designed specifically for the impact of dancing.

It was love at first sight.

I sat down on my bed. I was so excited, but then I felt like I might cry. I couldn't believe I'd actually won! It made me realise that not having much money didn't even matter, because if you really wanted something, you worked hard for it.

And that was just what I'd done.

Chapter Sixteen

I guess I don't have to tell you I was pretty excited for our final hip hop practice. I had my new high tops! Today we would also get our costumes for the dance.

At the start, when we were meant to be rich ladies, the girls were wearing black pants, white shirts and these big wide-brimmed hats that covered our faces. Then, while the boys came on and pretended to rob us, we quickly changed into our 'monster' outfits.

Everyone's was different. One girl was this crazy spider woman. Tove was a zombie, which she complained about at first, but then I think she really got into it. Another girl was a lizard demon, dressed in green from the top up.

I was meant to be a robot alien, or 'technology gone wrong', as Jay put it. My face was covered in metallic gold paint and my top half was all wrapped up in a silver and gold costume. (I could still move, of course.) It went really well with my purple, silver and gold high tops.

'Cool shoes,' Tove said to me, as we waited to begin practice.

'Thanks,' I said. 'They're from that Danceworks competition I won.'

Tove grinned. 'I'm really glad you got it. I can't wait to see when the shots come out!'

'I don't think I'll be able to look,' I said. 'I'll probably make everyone go blind!'

We got stuck into practice.

'Whoa, whoa, whoa, Ash,' Jay said at the end. 'You smashed it today! Smashin' Ash! What'd you have for breakfast this morning?'

'The usual,' I said.

'Must be the new kicks, eh?' said Jay with a wink. 'Miss Freestyle.'

It might have been. But some of it had come from me. I couldn't be more excited for my first hip hop performance.

I was going to be the best man-eating metallic robot alien ever!

***

Performance night! The energy was high and everyone was buzzing. I could smell jam doughnuts and hot chips. A makeshift stage had been set up near the Bayside city centre and a short way off there was a huge tent for all the dancers to get ready.

Inside were hay bales to sit on and make-shift mirrors. It was pretty packed. Everyone taking part in the showcase was there. Our hip hop crew were over in one corner getting our monster make-up done.

'Do I need to tease my hair more?' asked Tove.

It was weird to see her getting ready without Jasmine. Whenever we had a competition or performance, those two were always together somewhere, giggling or practising or doing their make-up. I sort of felt like, for this performance, I'd become Tove's Jasmine. But I didn't mind. Tove was pretty cool once you forgot she was Jasmine's best friend.

'Yep,' I said. 'Remember, the hat you have on at the start will squash your hair a bit.'

'Cool,' said Tove. 'Oh, your face is missing a bit of gold at the jaw. Do you want me to get ChiChi over or I can just do it?'

ChiChi was the lady responsible for painting us all up to look like monsters.

'You can just do it,' I said.

Tove grabbed a paintbrush and leaned over towards my face. She had painted-on scars with huge dark eyes and a bloody mouth. She looked awesome. If becoming a zombie was what it took for Tove to show some personality, then I was all for it!

'Hey,' said Benji, wandering over. 'You look like something I should run away from.'

'You look like something we want to chase,' I teased.

'You wanna go over our partner bit?' asked Benji.

'Sure,' I said. 'You finished?'

'Yep,' said Tove. 'All done.'

'Sorry,' said Benji, as we found a clear spot in the tent. 'I always get a bit nervous before performances. I like to go over everything.'

'I'd hate to imagine you and Paige before

your ballroom comps then,' I said. 'Paige gets the worst stage fright ever!'

'Yeah.' Benji laughed. 'But we're both so scared we kind of cancel each other out and just end up mucking around.' He shrugged. 'I don't mind ballroom, really. The dancing's cool. I just get teased a bit . . . with hip hop I can, I dunno, be myself.'

'I know the feeling,' I said.

I couldn't wait to feel the thrill of performing, waiting in the wings, listening for the music, walking out on stage and knowing that everyone was going to be watching me for the next five minutes.

Performing makes all the hard work worth it. I stop caring about what step comes next, or stuffing up, or forgetting where I'm supposed to be, or what everyone else is doing. I mean, I'm always aware of that, in the back of my mind, but the music just kind of takes over.

Benji and I practised our partner work, and then Jay called us all together. He joked around and told us how scarily amazing we looked.

'If anyone runs away screaming, you know you've done your job.' Jay grinned. 'I want to hear at least one crying baby!'

He was joking, of course, but Jay's good like that. By joking around, he took the pressure off us. He wanted us to do well, but to Jay it was more about loving the moment on stage and 'hitting it'.

'You can stuff up or fall on your bum and still kill it,' he said. 'Just roll.'

Soon enough the stage was dark and Jay sent the boys off to the side, ready for their entrance, and ushered us girls into our starting positions.

Time to hit it.

Chapter Seventeen

As soon as I heard the first lines of the song come over the speakers, and the drumbeats start, I felt like all my blood, bones and muscles had suddenly come to life.

Us girls began the dance, sitting around on couches and chairs, doing these popping, locking and isolation moves like we were rich and bored with nothing much to do. It was like we were in a trance.

Then we hit a sequence, dancing with our heads down, so our faces were shadowed by the huge hats we wore. This was meant to show that we were 'faceless', with no identity, but also to stop the audience from seeing the monster make-up we had on underneath.

Then Tove had to pretend she heard something (which was the boys trying to break in) and the pace sped up and we got more crazy.

Right at the end, we all threw our hats off, showing our monstrous faces to the audience, and dashed off stage.

It was panic round the back as shirts and hats went flying everywhere. The boys had 32 counts to do their sequence, and then the girls had another 32 counts to slowly creep on stage and start scaring them.

32 counts sounds like a lot, right? It isn't!

But we got there. We looked so awesome creeping onto the stage in our scary outfits.

I could see everyone out the corner of my eye. It must have looked so cool from the audience too, because the girls were in these brilliant colours swarming onto the stage and surrounding the boys, who were in their black and white outfits.

Then it got really funky. We all started dancing to the same choreography. We worked right into the ground, with our feet doing lots of jerking, walk-it-outs and smooth kick steps while our arms went crazy. Jay had us weaving in and out of patterns and formations all over the stage.

You know the thing I really love about hip hop? It comes back to Jay's favourite thing: hitting it.

Hitting the beat, hitting the move, hitting the feeling, hitting the choreography. When your move matches perfectly with whatever has just happened in the music, it feels like

BAM, got it! Your body brings the music to life.

When I began to do my partner work with Benji I could tell that he felt it too.

Don't get me wrong, I don't mind doing solos, but group dances are extra special. I guess it's kind of like watching art on the stage, because the choreographer has designed everything to look a certain way. And the energy on the stage is such a rush.

I've never had that much fun dancing, ever.

When the dance ended the boys finished up in a heap on the floor while we girls stood around them in a circle, laughing and jeering. Then Janet Jackson sang, '*I'm gone*,' and we spun on our heels and stalked off, leaving the boys in a muddled mess.

The applause started before we'd even left the stage.

Chapter Eighteen

After the performance we were allowed to go out and say hello to everybody who'd come to watch us. I love that moment after the dance, because often when people see you it's like they're looking at you in a whole new light.

It's a really nice feeling knowing you've done something that has wowed someone else.

'Ash, Ash, over here! Ashley!'

Ellie, Riley and Paige were standing off to the side, waving at me. When I got closer, Ellie ran up and gave me a huge hug.

'That was so cool, Ash!' she said. 'Oh my god, when you came on, it was so scary. You were great! And who would've thought Tove was into hip hop! Look, Jasmine, Daisy and Indianna are over there. I was spying on them during the performance. They looked super impressed.'

'I'd call it super jealous,' said Riley with a grin. 'You really showed them why you're the face of Freestyle. Leaving Dance Art was the best thing you ever did!'

They walked by then. Jasmine, Indianna and Daisy were all over Tove, telling her they 'knew she was a great hip hop dancer all along'. Tove turned round a little, rolled her eyes at me and then gave me a wave.

I waved back. I was glad she'd done something different from her friends and shone all on her own.

Ellie and Riley kept hugging me and wanting to know about the dance. Paige seemed a little distracted. She was looking over to where Benji was talking to his parents. It must have been strange to see him dance hip hop when she was so used to him acting all proper in ballroom! Finally she gave a little start and looked at me.

'That looked like heaps more fun than my last ballroom competition.' Paige grinned.

'You'll have to ask Benji about that,' I said. Paige blushed and looked down.

I thought maybe she had a little crush.

I spotted Bridget and Brimax near the back of the crowd and began leading the girls over to them.

'So, what next?' Ellie asked. 'Are you gonna be in video clips and stuff? Maybe you should learn to breakdance? I heard you get really bad back injuries, though.'

'AshFunk!' Brimax yelled when he saw me. 'There she is! What a performance!' He swept me up in a big hug. 'Man, I knew my boy Jay would get it out of you! And what about those kicks!'

'I think they helped a lot,' I said, smiling at Bridget.

'The shoes look great,' she said, giving me a kiss. 'So did you. Well done, Ash, I'm so proud. I didn't know my little sis could move like that!'

'Taught her everything she knows,' said Brimax.

'You did not,' said Bridget.

'Well, I was an inspiration, at least.'

Bridget went to play-hit him but he grabbed her and they started being all gross and lovey-dovey, so I looked away.

And I saw Mum and Dad.

They seemed a bit out of place, and they were still in their work clothes, but they were there, standing only a few metres away.

So they'd finally made it to one of my performances. They couldn't have picked a better one!

'You were beautiful, Ash,' said Mum. 'Or funky. Or . . . what's the right word? Whatever it is. You were perfect.'

'Totally cool,' said Dad, doing a move that was exactly the opposite.

I reached forward to give them a hug before I died of embarrassment.

But I wasn't really embarrassed. I was a big, fat, excited ball of happy.

I had a pair of the most amazing, delicious purple, silver and gold high tops, great new friends and was in my own dance crew.

And none of it would have ever been possible, unless I'd come to Silver Shoes!

Ashley Jenkyns

Full name: Ashley Adele Jenkyns

Nicknames: Ash, AshFunK

Age: 10

Favourite dance styles: Hip hop & funk

Best friend: Riley

Family: Mum, Dad, and my 18-year-old sister, Bridget

Favourite colour: Purple

Favourite food: Peanut butter sandwiches and jelly snakes

Favourite school subject: Science

Hobbies: Dancing, being in a dance crew, watching YouTube, playing practical jokes, volunteering with Coastwatch, swimming, snorkelling (in summer!)

What I want to be when I grow up: A dancer. Or a marine biologist.

Best dancing moment: When I finally tried hip hop and our crew performed at the festival

Things I love: Hanging out with Bridget and Brimax, big family dinners, watching hip hop battles and seeing all the different styles, making people laugh, sea animals (turtles are the best!), the beach, helping Dad in the garden and, of course, dancing!

How to do a Perfect Front Aerial

A front aerial is an acrobatic move, often found in hip hop dancing, in which a person performs a complete revolution of the body without touching the ground. Follow the movements in the illustration below for a front aerial that is both smooth and strong.

Tips

- Practise doing front walkovers and one-armed walkovers before you try to do a front aerial.
- Push up off the ground on your leading leg rather than out or forward. This will help you achieve the upward momentum you need.
- Don't forget to stand up straight at the end!

Glossary

Hey guys! I've made a list of some of the terms and moves that we use in hip hop class. There are a few acro terms here too, because Jay loves to put tricks into his choreography! Always use mats if you're trying anything new or hard, and remember that the move isn't always the most important thing, it's the 'flava' you put into your dancing. Have fun 'hitting it'!

Love, Ash

aerial a front walkover performed without any hands on the floor

b-boys/b-girls what you call dancers who breakdance

body roll when your whole body moves in a wave-like motion, most often starting with your head

boogaloo the aim is to dance so you look like you have no bones; it's a very loose movement that involves mostly rolling your hips, knees and legs

breaking breaking/breakdancing tends to be made up on the spot; you perform the moves at different levels, switching from uprock (performed while standing), to downrock (performed close to the floor), from power moves and acrobatics to freezes

choreographer the 'designer' of a dance routine. Choreography is all the moves, sequences, patterns and form that make up a dance.

cranking a crisscrossing bounce/jump travelling step, where your arms come up like you're riding a motorcycle

elbow stand this is like doing a handstand, but on your elbows, and usually one leg will be bent while the other is extended over your head

float a foot movement where you switch between putting weight on the toe and the heel so smoothly it looks like you are floating or gliding across the floor

floor sweep to sweep the floor in a circular motion with your foot and then move backwards on the other one

isolation moving one part of your body while you keep the rest still

jerking a movement where you bounce from one side to the other using your knees, keeping low to the ground, a 'groove'

kick step a low kick to the front followed by the opposite leg stepping out to the side

locking a series of locking movements where you perform a quick movement, lock into another position and then hold the last position for a beat. Usually your bottom half is relaxed while your top half does all the work!

popping this is quickly contracting and relaxing your muscles so it causes a jerk in your body. You usually perform it with other moves or poses.

reebok a travelling groove step where you rock from side to side using your feet, and your arms follow your body round

running man where one knee bends up to the front while the other shuffles back; you should stay in the one spot

side somersault a cartwheel performed without any hands on the floor

walk-it-out sitting low and keeping your knees bent, your legs twist from side to side while moving forward

wave where your body stays still while you hold your arms out so it looks like a wave is moving fluidly from one hand to the other

wop a bouncing groove where your knees bounce with the emphasis on the upbeat, and your arms and head swing left to right

About the Author

Samantha-Ellen Bound has been an actor, dancer, teacher, choreographer, author, bookseller, scriptwriter and many other things besides. She has published and won prizes for her short stories and scripts, but children's books are where her heart lies. Dancing is one of her most favourite things in the whole world. She splits her time between Tasmania, Melbourne, and living in her own head.

Can't get enough of Silver Shoes?
Be sure to check out Ellie's
story in *And All That Jazz*!
OUT NOW

Breaking Pointe
and
Dance Till You Drop
available April 2015